GOOD MORNING, BEAUTIFUL!

DISCOVERING YOUR TRUE BEAUTY

By: Katie Kemp

This book is dedicated to…

My mother, Pam,

Thank you for challenging me to pursue and chase my dreams.

I am grateful for your prayers.

My sister, Karissa,

Thank you for being my cheerleader and best friend.

You have wisdom beyond your years.

Table of Contents

~ Day 1 ~

You're Beautiful

I want to start this morning off by saying, "Good morning, beautiful!" Yes, the girl who stares bleary-eyed at you in the mirror every morning is gorgeous—even with smelly breath and no makeup.

When you look at yourself, you probably focus on every pore, wrinkle, stretch mark, pound, and blemish. You try to hide all those things by spending too much money on products that guarantee "perfect" results. Or maybe you've given up trying. You have accepted the lies the world has told you about yourself.

I'm guessing you compare yourself to other women too. Telling yourself, "If only I had what she had, then I ..." I have fallen into this trap far too often myself. I still sometimes wonder if I will ever feel comfortable in my own skin.

Here's the thing. You and I deserve so much more. We can choose to live every day with our heads held high, knowing we are beautiful, walking in confidence. Because here's what God says about us:

Let the king be enthralled by your beauty: honor him, for he is your Lord. (Psalm 45:11)

God is enthralled by your beauty! He gazes at you in amazement. You take His breath away.

If you could see yourself the way God sees you, you would no longer feel the need to compare yourself with anyone. How would your life change if you realized how beautiful you are though His eyes? If you lived every day looking at yourself through a filter of truth that says, "I am beautiful because I am loved by the King and He thinks I'm breathtaking!"

God created mankind in his own image, in the image of God he created them; male and female he created them. (Genesis 1:27)

You are created in the image of the King. True beauty is found when you discover the image of God within you, which transforms every flaw and molds you into something beautiful.

How beautiful you are, my darling! Oh, how beautiful! (Song of Songs 4:1)

Pause for a moment right now, look in the mirror, and tell yourself, "I am beautiful." If you need to, scream it at the top of your lungs! Put sticky notes all over your car. Set it as your screen saver. Before today ends, take some time to reflect on that truth.

You are altogether beautiful, my darling; there is no flaw in you. (Song of Songs 4:7)

Prayer

God, thank You for seeing me as beautiful. When I start to question who You created me to be, help me see myself through Your eyes. I am tired of letting the world define beauty for me. In You, I am beautiful simply because I am Your daughter. As I begin to see myself the way You see me, I will walk today in confidence because in Your eyes I'm breathtaking. In Jesus's name, amen.

~ Day 2 ~

Broken Hearts

Good morning, beautiful!

Are you feeling sad today? Maybe from some heartbreak buried deep inside? You don't want anyone to know, right? You want to be strong.

But experiencing pain doesn't mean you're weak. It means there is a place in your life that needs healing. It's okay to let out what you've been storing in your heart. Crying is a sign of courage because you're admitting you've been hurt and you're not afraid to find healing. So don't hold back the tears. Let them flow.

Jesus wept. (John 11:35)

Since even Jesus cried, it's good for us too. Instead of running from your pain, take it to Jesus. When you find yourself reliving a painful situation, ask Him to give you strength. He can help you find healing. He will remind you that you are chosen and you are loved.

The Lord is close to the brokenhearted and saves those who are crushed in spirit. (Psalm 34:18)

Throughout Scripture, the Greek word *Abba* is often used for God. Basically, it means "Daddy." When my heart is breaking, I long for my earthly daddy to hold me and tell me everything is going to be okay. But he's not always there to do that for me. We do, however, have a heavenly Father who is always with us. He sees your broken heart, your crushed spirit. When every day feels like a battle, He leans in close to you.

Is your present heartbreak too much for you to handle? It's not too much for God to handle. He will walk with you through this and you will overcome. Even if the circumstances do not change and the situation doesn't get better, you will be okay. Because when you focus your attention on God, you can find peace in His presence.

I have found that when I bring my heartbreak to God, healing sometimes comes from spending time in His word, journaling, or listening to music. Other times He leads me to healing by sharing what's going on in my life with a godly friend or seeking out Christian counselors to guide me though my pain in a healthy way.

Talk to God about your heartbreak and come up with a plan to find healing in your life. The pain you feel matters to God. He wants to help you find the healing you need.

He heals the brokenhearted and binds up their wounds. (Psalm 147:3)

Prayer

God, I am grateful that You are close to my broken heart, even though I don't always feel Your presence. As I focus on you, please fill me with peace. When my heart starts to ache, remind me to pause and ask You for strength. In Jesus's name, amen.

~ Day 3 ~

Be Still

Good morning, beautiful!

Life has a way of sneaking up on me, causing chaos, and filling my mind with doubt. Some days I feel like a whirlwind has snatched me up, and I'm not sure I will make it through. Can you relate?

Be still and know that I am God. (Psalm 46:10)

Every once in a while, we need to stop doing and just be still. When we fix our eyes on our Savior, it doesn't matter what life throws at us because God is in control. Our hope is not built on circumstances. It is found in knowing the one who has control of every situation.

Come to me, all who are weary and burdened, and I will give you rest. (Matthew 11:28)

Take a moment right now to remind yourself who God is and what that means for you.

Some days finding moments to be still is a challenge. When chaos hits, you may need to lock yourself in the bathroom for five minutes to refocus. Or stay in your car a little longer before stepping out. Or wake up five minutes earlier to enjoy a cup of coffee and a moment of stillness with the Lord. Whatever works for you, find a way to rest with God.

You will keep in perfect peace those whose minds are steadfast, because they trust in you. Trust in the Lord forever, for the Lord, the Lord himself, is the Rock eternal. (Isaiah 26:3–4)

When you take the time to be still and refocus on God, you can find peace as you place your trust in Him. Your heavenly Father will prove faithful every time.

Prayer

God, it is so easy for me to get overwhelmed and worried

about everything going on around me. Yet I don't have to fear, because You are in control every moment of every day. Help me take time today to be still and fix my eyes on You. In You I have all I need. In Jesus's name, amen.

~ Day 4 ~

Performance of Perfection

Good morning, beautiful!

I have a perfectionist tendency. I want everything in my life to be perfect, including myself. I push myself more than anyone else does. I work tirelessly to make sure everything around me stays in order. Sometimes I refuse to try something new just because I can't guarantee perfection.

My biggest fear is that someone will discover I'm not perfect. Or worse, that I'll find out I'm not perfect.

Do you struggle with this as well? Then let me tell you what I have to keep telling myself: It's okay to not be perfect. Because you have been given a great gift: grace. The unmerited and unearned kindness of God.

It is by grace that you have been saved, through faith—and this is not from yourselves, it is the gift of God—not by works, so that no one can boast. For we are God's handiwork, created in Christ Jesus to do good works, which

God prepared in advance for us to do. (Ephesians 2:8–10)

God chose you, and nothing you could ever do can change that. Giving yourself grace breaks the chains of performance. It sets you free to be the truest version of yourself. Give yourself permission to make mistakes and even fail sometimes. Allow yourself to release the unrealistic standards you've set. Your value is not defined by your performance.

When God created you, He said you were His handiwork. Even with all your "flaws," He still chooses you just as you are. You don't have to strive for His approval. The fingerprints of God are imprinted on you.

Prayer

God, thank You that I don't have to be perfect. Help me release the unrealistic standard of perfection I have set for myself and embrace grace. Remind me that I don't have to be perfect to gain Your love or the approval of others. I want to live in the grace and kindness You have shown me. In Jesus's name, amen.

~ Day 5 ~

Worry

Good morning, beautiful!

Worry can prevent us from falling asleep and wake us up in the middle of the night. We may be concerned about something small or what seems really big. Worry takes a seat in our minds and starts unpacking its suitcase like it's planning on staying a while. It is consuming, overwhelming, and exhausting.

But as daughters of the King, we can tell worry to pack its bags and hit the highway.

Are not two sparrows sold for a penny? Yet not one of them will fall to the ground outside your Father's care. And even the very hairs of your head are all numbered. So don't be afraid; you are worth more than many sparrows. (Matthew 10:29–31)

Even though worry may feel crippling and crushing right now, you won't fall to the ground because you are held in the

Father's hands. And you are worth so much to Him.

If God were sitting in your kitchen and having a cup of coffee with you right now, I think He would say, "Daughter, be still. I've got everything under control. Release your worry and fear. Let me carry the weight of this burden. I've got it. Trust me."

When this process gets difficult, ponder these powerful words from Scripture:

> We demolish arguments and every pretension that sets itself up against the knowledge of God, and we take captive every thought to make it obedient to Christ. (2 Corinthians 10:5)

To get freedom from fear and worry, we have to choose to put our thoughts into captivity and force them to see the truth of God. When you feel worry coming on, stop and pray, "Lord, these thoughts are not from You. I am taking captive every thought and making it obedient to You. Help me hear Your truth today."

When worry and fear try to sneak in, find a verse like the one above and recite it over and over. Think about the truths of God, not the worry.

Prayer

God, worry is trying to fill my mind. These thoughts are not from You. I am taking captive every thought and making it obedient to You. Help me focus on Your truth from John 14:27: "Peace I leave with you; my peace I give to you. I do not give as the world gives. Do not let your hearts be troubled and do not be afraid." I trust in You more than I trust in my fears. In Jesus's name, amen.

~ Day 6 ~

Overthinking

Good morning, beautiful!

Sometimes my overactive brain does not want to shut off. It overthinks and overanalyzes every little detail.

Last week, I texted "How are you doing?" to a friend and she didn't text me back. My brain went into overdrive. *What did I do? Did she take that text the wrong way? Is she mad at me? Will she ever talk to me again? Maybe she doesn't really like me. Have all these months of friendship been a lie? She's a really nice person. I hope we can work this out!*

All week these questions rolled through my head. Finally, I picked up the phone and called my friend. "Katie," she said, "thank you for checking on me. I'm fine. I just forgot to text you back. In the future, if I forget to reply, just text me again, okay?"

My silly brain had worked itself into a tizzy over nothing! I stressed out all week because I forgot about the one who holds my life in His hands.

If you can relate to my struggle, I want to share this verse with you:

> Our struggle is not against flesh and blood, but against the rulers, against the authorities, against the powers of this dark world and against the spiritual forces of evil in the heavenly realms. (Ephesians 6:12)

When we overthink things, a war begins in our minds. We can take back the battlefield by shutting off our overactive imagination and focusing on the one who has everything in control. He knows what He's doing and has our best interests at heart.

> We know that in all things God works for the good of those who love him, who have been called according to his purpose. (Romans 8:28)

Take that worry-filled brain captive and focus on the goodness of God. There's no need to overthink, because our God can work all things for our good!

Prayer

God, so often I try to control my situation instead of trusting in Your goodness and love for me. Remind me every day to take my thoughts captive and focus on You. Thank You, God, for being in complete control of every situation. In Jesus's name, amen.

~ Day 7 ~

You Are Worthy

Good morning, beautiful!

"Sticks and stones can break my bones, but words can never hurt me." I've always hated that phase because words do hurt. I have been on the receiving end of words that have caused me to question my worth, my value, and my identity. The words from the lips of others held me captive for so long, making me believe that I was unworthy of God's love. Maybe you've been trapped by the words of others too?

In the day-to-day moments, people may say things, intentionally or unintentionally, that cause us to forget our value. We base our opinions of ourselves on the comments of others and find ourselves lacking. Inadequate. When we're in that place, we forget that we are worthy of the love of our Savior … and worthy enough to return that love.

Here is what I want you to tell yourself right now: *I have value. I am the recipient of true love and I am worthy of giving love. I can be confident in who God created me to be.*

Your worth is far more than you could ever imagine. Your Father would move heaven and earth for you! That's how much you are worth to Him.

She is clothed with strength and dignity; she can laugh at the days to come. (Proverbs 31:25)

You are clothed each day with strength and dignity. God loves you fiercely.

I have loved you with an everlasting love; I have drawn you with unfailing kindness. (Jeremiah 31:3)

Your heavenly Father loves you with an everlasting love. He wants to draw you out of the shame of who you used to be so you can discover His unfailing kindness toward you.

So choose to live as you are: worthy of the love of your Father God. Be who you were created to be. Live free from the lies and embrace the strength and dignity within you.

Prayer

God, help me not to forget who I am. Daily remind me that You love me with an everlasting love. Show me the unfailing kindness You have toward me. Don't let me be afraid to embrace the true version of myself and live as the woman You have called me to be. Let me see myself through Your eyes today. In Jesus's name, amen.

~ Day 8 ~

Choose Victory

Good morning, beautiful!

Have you ever experienced a season of life when you felt like you were walking in constant defeat? Each second feels like a battle, and losing seems to happen a lot more often than winning. You try to do everything right. You keep giving it your all. You want a victory, but it feels impossible. You're not even sure you have a shot at making it through. What do you do when it feels like you are facing the impossible?

In 2 Chronicles chapter 20, we read the story of King Jehoshaphat and how he handled facing the impossible. A large army was coming to attack his people. While he was alarmed, he decided he must focus his attention on God.

Our God, will you not judge them? For we have no power to face this vast army that is attacking us. We do not know what to do, but our eyes are on you. (2 Chronicles 20:12)

We have all faced moments when the only thing we see is what we are up against. We can't see past the army ahead. When facing the impossible, we may not know what to do, but we know where to look. When we focus our attention on God, no matter how strong the army in front of us seems, the power of Almighty God is going into the battle with us.

He said: "Listen, King Jehoshaphat and all who live in Judah and Jerusalem! This is what the Lord says to you: Do not be afraid or discouraged because of this vast army. For the battle is not yours, but God's." (2 Chronicles 20:15)

Life won't always be easy. But we were not meant for this world. Our hearts long for eternity. Be courageous. Whether you see it or not, you already hold the victory through the power of Christ. You don't have to do this on your own. What feels to you like a defeat may be the exact thing God uses to set you up for victory.

God can bless us and use us to bless others even when we face the impossible.

Thanks be to God! He gives us the victory through our Lord Jesus Christ. Therefore, my dear brothers and sisters, stand firm. Let nothing move you. Always give yourselves fully to the work of the Lord, because you know that your labor in the Lord is not in vain. (1 Corinthians 15:57–58)

Prayer

God, help me to choose victory despite the circumstances that are coming against me. Fill me with Your power so I can stand firm as I continually seek You. When the day feels long, and I'm not sure I can make it, remind me to keep my eyes on You. Even when it seems like I am facing the impossible, I can be confident that victory is found in the power of Christ. In Jesus's name, amen.

~ Day 9 ~

Never Give Up

Good morning, beautiful!

Sometimes I am a whole lot better at quitting than persevering. When life gets hard, I would rather throw in the towel and give up. I want to take the easy way out because it seems simpler to walk away than to keep walking in the fire. However, I've been learning recently that the best things in life are worth fighting for, even if it means I will face the heat.

Are you facing something today that makes you feel like quitting? Don't give up. Fight for that relationship. Fight for that friend. Fight for what's right. Too much hangs in the balance for you to walk away.

God is within her, she will not fail; God will help her at break of day. (Psalm 46:5)

Most importantly, don't forget the one who is within you. God is holding tightly to you. He's got you and He will never let you go. He is really good at taking care of you. As long as you keep your eyes focused on Him, even when it is hard you can continue to persevere because He is with you.

God is our refuge and strength, an ever-present help in times of trouble. (Psalms 46:1)

God is not done with you. Depend on your Father to be your refuge and strength as you walk through this circumstance. He is all the help you need. The God who created the universe, and who knows every hair on your head, He is committed to this too. He is not giving up on you, but is with you and for you.

Your story is not over. Don't write an ending to a chapter just because it is hard. Press on to discover the beautiful story God is orchestrating for you. Continue doing what He has called you to do and don't give up.

Prayer

God, keep me moving forward, fighting for what I know is right. I trust You will sustain me as I follow You. You put me on this earth for a reason, and I don't want to waste a moment. Help me keep seeking You and never give up on what You have called me to do. In Jesus's name, amen.

~ Day 10 ~

Safe

Good morning, beautiful!

My family has fostered children for many years now. When a child comes into our home, they are typically looking for security. Although they may not say it verbally, their actions clearly show the question running around in their heads: "Is this a safe place?"

We all crave safety. We search for it in relationships, the places we go, the things we try to control, our jobs, our finances. Unintentionally, we try to create our own personal safety net to shield us from life's storms. We grasp for anything that resembles some form of protection.

I attempt to control everything in my life and others. Yet every day, no matter how hard I try, I never seem to achieve the security I've been looking for. When life begins to feel unstable, I long for somewhere I can go where I can feel steady again. I want someone to hold me tight and tell me everything is going to be okay.

The best place for us to find safety is in the arms of the

Father. When the world feels violent and filled with fear, lean into Him. Trust Him. He won't hurt you or let you down. He will provide you with a place where you can rest. The security you've been searching for is found in Him.

> He will cover you with his feathers, and under his wings you will find refuge; his faithfulness will be your shield and rampart. (Psalm 91:4)

God is saying to you, "You're safe with me. I won't let you go. I'm holding on to you and will protect you every step of every day. Rest in Me and find shelter in My gentle embrace."

> "Because [she] loves me," says the Lord, "I will rescue [her]; I will protect [her], for [she] acknowledges my name. [She] will call on me, and I will answer [her]; I will be with [her] in trouble, I will deliver [her] and honor [her]. (Psalm 91:14–15)

God can be trusted with your heart. He is there whenever you call. He is your safe place.

> Do not let your hearts be troubled. You believe in God;
>
> believe also in me. (John 14:1)

Prayer

God, I feel such freedom knowing I am protected in Your arms. I don't need to search for someone or something to run to because I can rest in You. I can trust You. You are my safe place. In Jesus's name, amen.

~ Day 11 ~

Heart of the Father

Good morning, beautiful!

There are days when I wonder, *Why on earth would God love someone like me? Does God even know I'm here? Does He care?* I really don't understand how the God who created the entire universe would want a personal relationship with someone like me.

One day, I asked God to help me understand His heart for me, and I came across this Scripture passage:

Lift up your eyes and look to the heavens; who created all these? He who brings out the starry host one by one and calls forth each of them by name. Because of his great power and mighty strength not one of them is missing. (Isaiah 40:26)

The God who calls each star by name and directs them to shine night after night knows my name. His heart is filled with love for me. And for you too.

It may seem silly, but sometimes I imagine God calling out

the stars, "Hey, Milky Way and Andromeda Galaxy, it's time to shine! See, there is this girl on earth—not to brag or anything, but she's pretty awesome. Yeah, I created her, and she is definitely one of my favorites. Well, they all are, but this one is special and she needs to be reminded that I love her. She needs to know *tonight* that I haven't forgotten her. So stars and galaxies, I want you to shine brighter than you ever have before. Do your thing so she can know I'm still here."

It blows my mind to think that the God who has yet to forget a single star in the sky hasn't forgotten me. Or you. (Read Luke 15.)

The truth is, it's crazy that God would love people like us. While I will probably never understand why He does, I know that as long as the stars keep shining, His love for me and for you will never fail.

Love is patient, love is kind. It does not envy, it does not boast, it is not proud. It does not dishonor others, it is not self seeking, it is not easily angered, it keeps no record of wrongs. Love does not delight in evil but rejoices with the truth. It always protects, always trusts, always hopes, always perseveres. Love never fails. (1 Corinthians 13:4–8)

Go look at the stars tonight. God wants to show you His love. This is the heart of the Father.

Prayer

God, thank You for showing me Your love in the stars that shine each night. When I start to question Your love for me, remind me that You haven't forgotten a single star in the sky and You won't forget me either. Help me to see myself through Your eyes and remind me that You love me unconditionally. In Jesus's name, amen.

~ Day 12 ~

Run to Your Anchor

Good morning, beautiful!

When things happen that feel overwhelming and out of my control, I have a tendency to run to a friend. I want her to anchor me and keep me steady amid the storm. In my search for peace, I often turn to friends before I turn to God.

Recently, God cut the ropes on every anchor I set that wasn't in Him. Some friendships that ended because they led me away from God. People who were once a daily part of my life weren't there anymore. Some moved to different states for job opportunities and with others we just lost contact. It's scary to watch the people you once ran to for security suddenly disappear.

I asked God, "Why?" I heard Him say, "I want you to realize that I am all you need and you can anchor in Me."

When God made His promise to Abraham, since there was no one greater for him to swear by, he swore by himself, saying, "I will surely bless you and give you many descendants." And so after waiting patiently, Abraham received what was promised. People swear by someone greater than themselves, and the oath confirms what is said and puts an end to all argument. Because God wanted to make the unchanging nature of his purpose very clear to the heirs of what was promised, he confirmed it with an oath. God did this so that, by two unchangeable things in which it is impossible for God to lie, we who have *fled* to take hold of the hope set before us may be greatly encouraged. *We have this hope as an anchor for the soul, firm and secure.* It enters the inner sanctuary behind the curtain, where our forerunner, Jesus, has entered on our behalf. He has become a high priest forever, in the order of Melchizedek. (Hebrews 6:13–20, emphasis mine)

Beautiful one, who do you run to when you need an anchor? Are you trying to pull peace into your life or are you seeking peace in the Father? God will fulfill every promise, and He will always be by your side. He wants you to look beyond the circumstances and take hold of hope.

Having friends is important, and it's okay to lean on others for wisdom and guidance. God puts people in our lives as gifts to encourage and support us. However, when you notice yourself running every problem by a person before you consult God first, be cautious. You may have unintentionally created an anchor in a person rather than God.

Run to God first and tell Him the desires and requests of your heart. Let Him show you that He is all you need. Let Him anchor your soul into His unfailing love.

Prayer

God, far too often I run to people or things to try to steady me. I am searching for a place that is firm and secure … and all along it's been You. Cut the ropes to all the anchors in my life that don't need to be there. Help me to anchor my soul in Your hope first, and then enable me to see the people and things around me as gifts from You. In Jesus's name, amen.

~ Day 13 ~

I Want You

Good morning, beautiful!

Recently, I started praying, "God, I want what You want more than what I want." The more I pray this prayer, the harder it gets.

To begin with, I have to discern the difference between what I want, what I think God wants, and what God really wants. Typically, when I pray this prayer, I'm asking God for what I want and what I think God wants for me. If I'm being honest, I don't really want what God wants unless it lines up with my plans.

Because let's be real—wanting what God wants means loving the people who are hard to love. It means stepping out of my comfort zone. Doing what He has called me to do is going to cost me something. It's not going to make my life easier. It will probably make it a lot more complicated.

Praying this prayer resulted in my ending a dating relationship with a great guy because we both felt God was calling us in different directions.

This prayer also caused a job change. It cost me a lot, and I had to give up things I thought I wanted.

But I kept praying it. And it has taught me a great deal about the character of God as a good Father. This prayer has made me more intentional about loving people well. And it has enabled me to forgive childhood wounds.

As a kid, I was deathly allergic to peanuts. One day, as I watched my dad eating a Reese's peanut butter cup, I begged, "Daddy, I want one! Please?" But he couldn't give it to me because it would have been deadly for me. It wasn't easy to tell his little girl no. But he understood that by withholding what I wanted he was protecting me from a danger I couldn't see.

As I pray this prayer, God doesn't always give me what I want. But He always gives me what I need, and He protects me from dangers I can't see.

When it comes right down to it, what I want—and need—more than anything is His presence. If letting go of what I want gives me a glimpse of His presence, that's what I really want!

Lord, walking in the way of your laws, we wait for you; your name and renown are the desire of our hearts. My soul yearns for you in the night; in the morning my spirit longs for you. When your judgements come upon the earth, the people of the world learn righteousness. (Isaiah 26:8–9)

I challenge you to boldly pray, "God, I want what You want more than what I want." As you align your desires with His, the longing of your heart will be for His name and His renown.

Prayer

God, I want what You want more than what I want. The desire of my heart is to follow You in everything. I long to fall in love with You as much as You have fallen in love with me. May my heart grow to love You more each day. Thank You for loving me with a love that never ends. In Jesus's name, amen.

~ Day 14 ~

Lost

Good morning, beautiful!

I have a confession to make. I get lost ... a lot. I can't tell north from south or east from west. I don't travel anywhere without GPS.

In addition to my incredible track record of being "directionally challenged," I have a knack for getting lost spiritually. I try to grow in my relationship with God, but I end up feeling lost in the middle of nowhere. I wonder, *How did I get here?* I wish it was as easy to get found as it was to get lost.

Do you feel that way sometimes? How about we get found together?

Come near to God and he will come near to you. (James 4:8)

The extent to which you draw close to God will be the extent He draws close to you. God wants to be in your life, but He's not going to force His way in.

Relationship are a two-way street. When God seems distant in my life and I feel lost, there is a good chance I'm the one who moved.

Getting found may not be as hard as you think, but it does require sacrifice. It takes humility to say, "God, I've drifted. But now I'm focusing my eyes on You and choosing to come near to You."

Identify the areas in your life that are causing you to move away from God. It may be a relationship, a television show, or even unnecessary priorities in your schedule. Then do whatever it takes to remove those things and draw closer to God by spending time with Him instead.

This is not a quick fix. The process will take time. Even if you still feel lost tomorrow, next week, or next month, choose to keep trusting God.

One day, I was driving behind a friend who was leading me to a place I had never been. At one point she called my cell phone and asked, "Do you trust me to lead you where I told we'd go?"

"Of course," I replied. "You've been there before."

"Do you have your GPS on?" she asked.

"No," I said. "I turned it off because I am following you."

Sometimes I may say I'm trusting God to lead me, but I get impatient and turn on my spiritual GPS and ask Him to follow me. I start trying to control the situation. Then I wonder why I can't find my way out.

I recently gave God my five-year plan of where I wanted to be in life and what I expected Him to do for me. I kept getting frustrated when doors I wanted open kept closing.

When I finally asked God what He was trying to teach me in this season, it hit me that God couldn't teach me anything. I was too busy trying to do my own things and telling God, "I have a great plan! Follow me!" I was no longer taking time to rest, seek His will for my life, and trust that His plans for me are good.

God can't lead you from where you are now if you keep asking Him to follow you. Stop striving by your own strength. Put your complete trust in God and submit everything to Him. Follow His GPS, not yours. You'll find your way out faster than you think.

Trust in the Lord with all your heart and lean not on your own understanding; in all your ways submit to him and he will make your paths straight. (Proverbs 3:5–6)

Prayer

God, I have let my heart drift from You. But I am choosing now to focus on You. I don't know what to do about my situation. But I trust You with every detail and I release my desire for control. Help me to follow You, even in what feels like the middle of nowhere. Make my paths straight and lead me where You are calling me to be. In Jesus's name, amen.

~ Day 15 ~

Live to the Fullest

Good morning, beautiful!

When was the last time you let yourself laugh? A belly-roll, almost pee-in-your-pants laugh? If you can't remember, it's been too long.

The past few months I let myself get so caught up in the stress and disappointments of life I became too paralyzed to laugh. I poured my heart and soul into work, hoping a glimpse of success would free me. Instead I become full of bitterness.

Have you been trying to numb the pain for so long that you have forgotten to live? Have you let the desire for achievements tomorrow drive you today? Stop. Take a breath. Live in this moment. Don't let worries drag you down. Enjoy the glorious life God has given you. Enjoy today.

The thief comes only to steal and kill and destroy; I have come that they may have life, and have it to the full. (John 10:10)

God made you to live life to the fullest. He doesn't want you to drag by in despair. Every day is a reminder that you are blessed.

> You make known to me the path of life; you will fill me with joy in your presence, with eternal pleasures at your right hand. (Psalms 16:11)

Life is but a vapor. Tomorrow is not promised. So own this moment. Be present with the people around you now. Make today count.

This morning, I picked vegetables from my garden. I sat at the dinner table and laughed with my family. At the end of the day I told my little brother a bedtime story. There was nothing extraordinary about today. But I set aside my worries and my agenda to enjoy my loved ones. I chose to live in the moment and laugh through the ups and downs.

Do something fun today. Go on an adventure. Laugh. Take a deep breath and live life to the fullest.

Prayer

God, I'm sorry for working so hard to build my own kingdom that I forgot to put You first. Forgive me for letting myself get so focused on myself that I neglect to enjoy every blessing You have given me. Help me pay attention to the little moments today and to laugh. Remind me that happiness is found in happenings, but joy is found in You. Keep me from running so fast that I don't live the life You've given me to the fullest. Thank You for blessing me. In Jesus's name, amen.

~ Day 16 ~

Martha

Good morning, beautiful!

By nature, I make a much better Martha than Mary. (See Luke 10:38–42.) I try so hard to earn love from others and from God. I feel like the more I do, the more acceptance I will receive, the more others will approve of me, and the more valued I will be. But it's a never-ending battle, because there is always so much to do and I feel like I need to tackle it all.

A mentor once helped me identify this problem by asking me, "Are you working *for* God's love or working *from* God's love?"

Have you been there? Are you there now? Working hard and waiting for someone to tell you, "Good job"? Even if you hear those coveted words, it still doesn't feel like enough, so you work harder. Your brain is fried. People at work are telling you to go home. People at home are telling you to slow down. But you can't, because if you stop, people won't love you, right?

"Martha, Martha," the Lord answered, "you are worried and

upset about many things, but few are needed—or indeed only one. Mary has chosen what is better and it will not be taken from her." (Luke 10:41–42)

I picture Jesus's eyes gazing at His beautiful one, wishing she could see herself the way He did. I imagine Jesus said this phrase in almost a whisper, with kindness mixed with a hint of sadness. He was letting Martha know, maybe for the first time, that it was okay to stop doing because she would be accepted for who she was, not for what she did.

You too are loved, accepted, valued, and chosen. Jesus wants you to come and sit at His feet. To rest. To know that you are enough. To know that you are loved for yourself. You are not defined by what you do or accomplish. You are a beautifully chosen daughter of the King. Rest and let His love cover you. Don't leave until you believe you are enough just as you are.

Prayer

God, help me find freedom from doing in order to earn love and realize that I am loved for myself. Speak Your truth over me today, the truth that says I am loved, accepted, valued, and chosen for simply being me. You love me just as I am. I choose to sit at Your feet and rest. I want to slow down long enough to understand that Your love for me is not based on what I do. Thank You for giving me Your unconditional love and for loving me with no strings attached. In Jesus's name, amen.

~ Day 17 ~

Face the Pain

Good morning, beautiful!

I am not a fan of pain, physical or emotional. I try to avoid it at all cost. If I can't avoid it, I try to hide it. If I can't hide it, I try to ignore it. Or pretend I don't feel it. The longer I've continued this behavior, the more I realized how self-sabotaging it can be.

Are you facing heartbreak, insecurity, rejection, or doubts today? I want to encourage you to do something brave. Choose to face the pain. Stop running from it or trying to hide it. Walk straight toward it. Let yourself feel the pain you've been trying to avoid for so long.

I know it's hard. But you can't find healing until you admit there's a problem. But don't go alone. Bring two people with you: a wise, godly, close friend and Jesus.

Two are better than one; because they have a good return for their labor: if either of them falls down, one can help the other up. But pity anyone who falls and has no one to help them up. (Ecclesiastes 4:9–10)

You need a friend to help you walk through this and to help you up if you fall. So be brave and tell her what's going on. Everything. She will still love you.

When hard pressed, I cried to the Lord; he brought me into a spacious place. The Lord is with me; I will not be afraid. What can mere mortals do to me? The Lord is my helper. I look in triumph on my enemies. (Psalm 118:5–7)

Don't forget to bring Jesus with you too. He wants to help you, and He wants to fill you with peace so you don't have to be afraid. If you let Him walk with you through this, Jesus can set you free. With Him, you can be braver than you ever imagined.

Prayer

God, help me be brave today. I don't want this pain to torment me any longer. I'm ready to face it head on and win. Lead me to the friend You want me to invite to come into this with me.

Let me be brave enough to say yes to a counselor if that's what this journey requires. I am willing to do the hard work to become a healthier version of who You created me to be. In Jesus's name, amen.

~ Day 18 ~

Great Job

Good morning, beautiful!

The other day I almost quit my job because I thought I wasn't qualified enough to do it. I didn't do anything wrong. No one told me I was doing a bad job. In fact, that morning my boss told me he was proud of my work. But I put so much pressure on myself to be better, I never allowed myself to stop and celebrate the things I had accomplished. I almost gave up because I never gave myself permission to tell myself, "Great job!"

Dear friend, celebrate what you've done. You are a phenomenal worker, friend, sister, daughter, wife, mom. You are doing a remarkable job of simply being you.

It's easy to get so caught up in day-to-day life that we discount who we are and what we do. We let simple mistakes cloud our judgment and we beat ourselves up.

Think of something you did today that you can be proud of and tell yourself, "Great job!" Even if all you did was get out of bed, that is something to celebrate.

Give yourself credit for the amazing things God has allowed you to do and be a part of.

I thank my God every time I remember you. In all my prayers for all of you, I always pray with joy because of your partnership in the gospel from the first day till now, being confident of this, that he who began a good work in you will carry it on to completion until the day of Christ Jesus. (Philippians 1:3–6)

I am thankful for you. My heart is filled with joy because we are serving an amazing God together. I'm glad we're on the same team. Because you are valuable. You are incredible. God knows you are awesome!

Keep it up, friend. You're doing a great job.

Prayer

God, thank You for letting me serve You in so many ways. For too long I have believed the lies that I am not good enough and never will be. Yet You are proud of me, so I can be proud of myself.

I don't want to keep comparing myself to others or living by my mistakes. Today let me see the good works You are doing in me. Thank You for allowing me to be part of the Great Commission. Thank You for using me to reach this world for Christ. In Jesus's name, amen.

~ Day 19 ~

Do It Scared

Good morning, beautiful!

Is God calling you to do something, but you've been running from it? Is there an issue you need to stand up for, but you're hiding behind fear? Is there an encouragement you need to share, but you're keeping it locked inside? Is there someone you need to ask forgiveness from, but pride is standing in the way? What is the thing you know you need to do, but you are afraid to do it?

Do it anyway! Courage is choosing to do something even though it scares you. Your first attempt (or first several attempts) may not be perfect. But the results will eventually be worth the effort.

I came to you in weakness with great fear and trembling. My message and my preaching were not with wise and persuasive words, but with a demonstration of the Spirit's power, so that your faith might not rest on human wisdom, but on God's power. (1 Corinthians 2:3–5)

In the midst of his fear and inadequacies, the apostle Paul preached the message of the gospel. He discovered that when we do what God calls us to do, He shows up. I can't, but my God can! Give the people around you a chance to see how God's power can show up despite your weaknesses.

Step out of your comfort zone and take a leap of faith. Will you fail? Possibly. But maybe you'll succeed. Don't miss out on seeing God's power at work in you. Your faith will grow like never before.

I often pray, "God, give me the courage to try and the grace to fail." I challenge you to pray that over yourself. Then watch Him work in and through you.

Prayer

God, today I choose to step out in faith and do that thing You have been calling me to do. I pray that You would give me the courage to take this leap of faith. Let me see Your power at work in me. Give me the courage to try and the grace to fail. Remind me that Your power is stronger than any obstacle or failure I will face. Today, God, I choose to just do it scared. In Jesus's name, amen.

~ Day 20 ~

Shame

Good morning, beautiful!

Are you carrying a load of shame on your shoulders? Are you ashamed of your weight? A relationship that ended badly? A mistake you made? The lack of time you've made for others and for God? Do you hear a voice in your head screaming, "You are a failure"?

Jesus went to the Mount of Olives. At dawn he appeared again in the temple courts, where all the people gathered around him, and he sat down to teach them. The teachers of the law and the Pharisees brought in a woman caught in adultery. They made her stand before the group and said to Jesus, "Teacher, this woman was caught in the act of adultery. In the Law Moses commanded us to stone such women. Now what do you say?" They were using this question as a trap, in order to have a basis for accusing him.

But Jesus bent down and started to write on the

ground with his finger. When they kept on questioning him, he straightened up and said to them, "Let any one of you who is without sin be the first to throw a stone at her." Again he stooped down and wrote on the ground.

At this, those who heard began to go away one at a time, the older ones first, until only Jesus was left, with the woman still standing there. Jesus straightened up and asked her, "Woman, where are they? Has no one condemned you?"

"No one, sir," she said.

"Then neither do I condemn you," Jesus declared. "Go now and leave your life of sin." (John 8:1–11)

This woman felt complete shame. She had just been caught in one of the worst mistakes she ever made. The man she'd slept with was gone, leaving her exposed. She must have thought, *I will never be loved again. I can never be forgiven. I deserve every stone that is about to be pelted at my head.*

Then the unimaginable happens. Her accusers take her to Jesus. The shame is unbearable. She wishes she could hide.

The railings against her grow silent. She looks up and

everyone is gone. Jesus stands alone before her.

What will He do? Kill her? Use her? Shame her?

He says softly, "I forgive you."

Why would He do that? She deserves to die.

Then He says, "Neither do I condemn you. ... Go now and leave your life of sin" (John 8:11).

She is forgiven She can leave her life of sin and get a fresh start.

In that moment this woman's identity changed from adulterous to loved.

I am forgiven.

I have a new story.

I am a child of God.

Don't let the thoughts in your head overshadow the truth of God. Shame has no place here. Just because you made a mistake or a wrong decision, your story doesn't end there. God's grace is enough. There is nothing you can do that He can't forgive. You are not condemned. It's time to leave your sin behind and move into your new story.

God demonstrates his own love for us in this: while we were still sinners, Christ died for us. (Romans 5:8)

Where sin increased, grace increased all the more, so that, just as sin reigned in death, so also grace might reign through righteousness to bring eternal life through Jesus Christ our Lord. (Romans 5:20–21)

Forgive yourself. Let go of the shame you've placed on your shoulders. Accept the gift of forgiveness that God has given you and live in the freedom of grace. Don't dwell on past mistakes. Stop trying to figure out what you could have done differently. Just breathe. Release the shame and grab hold of grace.

When you hear the voice of shame trying to sneak back into your mind, tell it, "Shame, you are not welcome here! I am a daughter of God. My mistakes do not define me because the forgiveness of my heavenly Father has redeemed me."

Shame has no place in you. You are forgiven. You are free.

Prayer

God, I have carried this shame for so long, it has become a chain that confines me. I have allowed it to consume my mind and shape my decisions. Help me to release the shame and embrace grace. Remind me that "where sin increased, grace increased all the more, so that, just as sin reigned in death, so also grace might reign through righteousness to bring eternal life through Jesus Christ our Lord" (Romans 5:20–21). My mistakes don't define me. You love me and I am forgiven. When shame tries to take root inside my mind, I will tell it, "I am a daughter of God, forgiven through grace." Your forgiveness has redeemed me. Thank You for freeing me from shame and filling me with grace. In Jesus's name, amen.

~ Day 21 ~

Comparison

Good morning, beautiful!

Do you ever secretly wish someone else could fail and watch you succeed? I'm guilty of the comparison trap. Measuring myself against other people's success is a never-ending competition in a game the opponent doesn't even know she's playing.

Stop comparing yourself to others. Focus on the value of who God created you to be. There is no one in this world who can do a better job of being you than *you*. If you get caught up in comparison, you'll miss what God wants to do in you.

A heart at peace gives life to the body, but envy rots the bones. (Proverbs 14:30)

You will never find peace if you are constantly looking to others to find your worth. No one wins in comparison. Discover the things you are great at.

What makes you come alive? Do those things to the best of your ability. And let others succeed at what they do well. Celebrate the gifts God has given you and them.

Just because your gifts and talents are different from those of others doesn't mean either of you is less valuable. God uniquely wired you to do great things and He uniquely wired them to do great things. Do you well, and let God use you where He has called you. Your life has purpose and meaning. Don't focus so much on someone else's purpose that you miss out on yours.

Prayer

God, I have played the comparison game too many times. Remind me that You made me with a specific purpose, just as You made others with their specific purposes. Help me celebrate the gifts You have given them and faithfully use the gifts You have given me. Let me be the cheerleader who encourages others to reach the next level while I do what You called me to do. Open the right doors for me to serve You to the best of my ability and fulfill the great purpose and plan You have for me. Thank You for letting me be part of this great story and thank You for letting others have a part as well. Our world is better because we all get the chance to serve You together.

In Jesus's name, amen.

~ Day 22 ~

Proud

Good morning, beautiful!

Your heavenly Father is proud of you. Not for what you have done or what you will do. He is proud because you were made in His image. He is pleased with the amazing woman you have been from the very start.

If you strip away your work title, family, accomplishments, degrees, money, house, car, and opportunities, God is still proud of you. Even if you fail, God is proud of you. His love isn't based on what you have or what you do but who you are in Him: His daughter. He loves you relentlessly and wants to show you off to the whole world. You can face today fearless because your Daddy is proud of who He created you to be.

This is what the Lord says—he who created you, Jacob, he who formed you, Israel: "Do not fear, for I have redeemed you; I have summoned you by name; you are mine. When you pass through the waters, I will be with you; and when you walk through the rivers, they will not sweep over you. When you walk through the fire, you will not be burned; the flames will not set you ablaze. For I am the Lord your God, the Holy One of Israel, your Savior; I give Egypt for your ransom, Cush and Seba in your stead. Since you are precious and honored in my sight, and because I love you, I will give people in exchange for you, nations in exchange for your life." (Isaiah 43:1–4)

You are redeemed, summoned by name. No matter what hardship or difficulty may come your way, you are precious and honored in His sight. He would move heaven and earth to prove His love for you. He would give everything for you. In fact, He did when He gave His Son.

God so loved the world that he gave his one and only Son, that whoever believes in him shall not perish but have eternal life. For God did not send his Son into the world to condemn the world, but the save the world through him. (John 3:16–17)

You can't earn His love. You don't deserve it. But He gave it anyway because He wanted to show you that you are worth fighting for. You are His beautiful daughter and He loves you relentlessly.

Prayer

God, sometimes I'm not proud of myself. Yet You say I am redeemed, summoned, precious, and honored. I am loved not for what I do but for who I am in You. Help me remove my identity from what I do and place it on who I am in Christ. Ultimate freedom is found in You. Thank You for loving me even though I don't deserve it and for reminding me that You are proud of me through it all. In Jesus's name, amen.

~ Day 23 ~

Weak Flesh

Good morning, beautiful!

Have you heard the expression "The Spirit is willing, but the flesh is weak"? Did you know that comes directly from the Bible?

Watch and pray so that you will not fall into temptation. The Spirit is willing, but the flesh is weak. (Mark 14:38)

That statement hits the nail on the head so personally it makes my heart ache. I desire to follow Christ and live out the plan He has for me, but my flesh fights against that plan over and over. I often desire my own glory rather than the glory of His great name. I want to make myself known rather than making Him known. I try to be humble, yet pride rips through my bones. I strive to do good on my own but keep falling short. My mind tells me to quit before I get in over my head, to give up because I'm not strong enough to win the battle, to run because I don't want to look like a failure.

What if there's a better way? The answer is right in front of us. We simply need to live out the verse above.

It's time for us to declare that we will not remain captive to our sins. In order for freedom to take root in our hearts, we need to pray as if our lives depended on it, because they do. We must strengthen our spirits so our flesh will fail us no more. If we release the guilt we place on ourselves, we can grab hold of the faithfulness of God.

He said to me, "My grace is sufficient for you, for my power is made perfect in weakness." Therefore I will boast all the more gladly about my weaknesses, so that Christ's power may rest on me. That is why, for Christ's sake, I delight in weakness, in insults, in hardships, in persecutions, in difficulties. For when I am weak, then I am strong. (2 Corinthians 12:9–10)

We humans have weaknesses and blind spots. Yet God's grace is sufficient and His power is made perfect in our weakness. He will make us strong if we put in the work of prayer.

First Thessalonians 5:17 says we are to "pray continually."

We must never stop praying, no matter the circumstance.

Pray as if there is no tomorrow. Through your prayers you will see how God's grace is sufficient and how His power is made perfect despite your weak flesh.

Prayer

God, I come before You knowing my flesh is weak. It longs after the things of this world. It wants to build my kingdom rather than Yours. Help me to pray without ceasing. May my life be built on prayer and my focus be less of me and more of You. Help me to be on high alert for You and against the things that seek to turn my attention away from You. Strengthen my spirit in You. In Jesus's name, amen.

~ Day 24 ~

Kill the Monster

Good morning, beautiful!

There is a monster in my mind that lies to me. It makes me walk in defeat because it makes me feel like I will never be good enough. I have given this monster so much power over me that I question every decision I make.

Do you have a monster like that in your mind too? Philippians 4:7–8 tells us the easy way to rid our minds of it.

The peace of God, which transcends all understanding, will guard your hearts and your mind in Christ Jesus. Finally, brothers and sisters, whatever is true, whatever is noble, whatever is right, whatever is pure, whatever is lovely, whatever is admirable, if anything is excellent or praiseworthy think about such things.

The monster in my mind screams loudest when I'm not intentional about taking my thoughts captive. I let my mind run wild and ask *What if?* and *What should I have done differently?*

A failure to fix my attention on what is true, noble, right, pure, lovely, admirable, and praiseworthy, often causes the loss of the battle. However, when I focus on the goodness and faithfulness of God, the negative voices in my head are silenced. We have the power to mute the lies by praising Jesus.

John 15 tells us God cuts off the branches in our lives that aren't bearing fruit. And He prunes the ones that do so they can become more fruitful.

You are already clean because of the word I have spoken to you. (John 15:3)

God wants to remove all the bad habits and hang-ups that are holding you back. It may be a slow and sometimes painful process, but He can move you from where you are now to where He has called you to be.

When the monster shows up, remind yourself of the words God has spoken over you. Think about what is true and praise the name of Jesus.

Prayer

God, lies consume my mind's attention when my focus is not on You. Help me to kill the monster I have allowed to dwell in my brain. May I only think of things that are true, noble, right, pure, lovely, admirable, excellent, or praiseworthy. I take my thoughts captive and surrender them to You. Thank You for Your peace, which transcends all understanding. Let it guard my heart today as I focus my mind on You. In Jesus's name, amen.

~ Day 25 ~

Refined

Good morning, beautiful!

God's Word says He works all things for good (Romans 8:28). But life doesn't always feel good. There are days when I seriously consider throwing in the towel because walking away from God and my faith would be so much easier.

But would it really? Life is going to happen whether or not I let God play a part in the story. And I don't want to live a single day without Him.

When gold is refined, it is heated and put under intense pressure to remove impurities. This allows the gold to be formed to its purest state. What if we used the difficulties in our lives to allow God to refine us rather than blaming Him for them?

Create in me a pure heart, O God, and renew a steadfast spirit within me. (Psalm 51:10)

What if God is using this time of pain to refine you, to create the purest version of yourself? Maybe what you're facing is hard because impurities are being removed. Perhaps this situation is shaping you into the image of who God created you to be.

I don't believe God intends for His children to suffer. But we live in a broken world. Hardship is going to show up from time to time. Why not lean into what's causing you the most pain and let God use it to further refine you? He can use our most challenging moments to make something beautiful.

This third I will put into the fire; I will refine them like silver and test them like gold. They will call on my name and I will answer them; I will say, "They are my people," and they will say, "The Lord is our God." (Zechariah 13:9)

In the midst of pain, God loves us. As we let Him, He uses the pain to purify us, creating in each of us a pure heart that resembles His.

When struggles come, instead of asking, "God, why is this so hard?" we can ask, "God, what in me needs to be purified?"

Prayer

God, do You have a purpose for my pain? Can You use the difficult moments in my life to purify me? I want You to create in me a pure heart and renew a steadfast spirit within me so I can walk through the fire and not be burned. I want my heart to resemble Yours. And that can only happen if I willingly surrender and let you purify and refine me. I will declare that the Lord is my God! In Jesus's name, amen.

~ Day 26 ~

God Knows What You Need

Good morning, beautiful!

God knows exactly what you need. So He can provide for your needs. You don't have to do anything but surrender to Him.

That may seem obvious, but it's something I easily forget.

Earlier this month I sat alone on my grandma's front porch, crying because I was burnt out on ministry and about to face an incredibly busy week. I was ready to throw in the towel and quit, and I didn't have a problem telling God that. In less than twenty-four hours, I developed bronchitis. I spent the next week in bed doing nothing. My team had to pick up the workload while I rested.

That respite was important for more than just physical reasons. I had to be reminded that God can and will take care of me. In that portion of time where I didn't have anyone depending on me to get the job done, I discovered it's okay to say no to things so I can take care of myself emotionally, physically, and spiritually.

God doesn't need me, but He allows me to play a role in His bigger story. Quitting wasn't the answer. I just needed a time of rest to realign my heart with His. Most importantly, I surrendered my agenda for His will.

Have you forgotten that God knows what you need? Even if you have, God hasn't forgotten about you.

My God will meet all your needs according to the riches of his glory in Christ Jesus. (Philippians 4:19)

God will give you what you *need* to face whatever you're going through. Tell Him what you're feeling, surrender your weakness and your agenda, and trust that He will meet you right where you are and He will provide. Notice Paul doesn't say *wants*. God doesn't always give us what we want. It is just like any good parent won't give their kids exactly what they want all the time. It would be unhealthy to feed them ice cream at every meal when they need to eat broccoli. I think God is similar. He may withhold what we want so he can lead us to what is vitally important. A relationship with Him.

What you're facing is no surprise to God. He knew this was coming, and He will give you exactly what you need to face today.

Prayer

God, You know what I'm up against today and how it is wearing me down. Would You meet me here and remind me that You know what I need better than I do? I can have peace because You will carry me through. You are still in control. Thank You that You provide and take care of me each day. Help me slow down enough to surrender. Thank You for being bigger than I can ever imagine. In Jesus's name, amen.

~ Day 27 ~

Open-Handed

Good morning, beautiful!

I'm not very good at letting go. I want to control every situation. When I can't, I feel helpless. I'm discovering maybe that's where I'm supposed to be. When I let go, Jesus shows up, but the tighter I hold on, the further away He seems to be. When I feel helpless, He shows me I can be helped. I just have to open my hands.

Beautiful one, remain open-handed. The tighter you clench on to life, the less you can truly hold on to. Control is a false security. Only when you open your hands that you can grab ahold of the hope you need.

Letting go is hard. I often release and then try to reach again for control. In those moments the question becomes *Do I really believe God will take care of me?* I know He can, but will He choose to do it? When I let go I show that I trust the story He is writing, even if it has a different ending than I hoped.

Whom do you trust—yourself or your heavenly Father?

Overhearing what they said, Jesus told him, "Don't be afraid, just believe." (Mark 5:36)

In Mark 5:21–43 you can read the story of Jairus, a synagogue leader, whose daughter died after he asked Jesus to come and heal her. When he heard that news, it would have been easy for him to blame Jesus for taking so long to get there. Instead Jairus held on to the words of Jesus: "Don't be afraid, just believe." He trusted Jesus even though he didn't know how his story would end. If he hadn't shown that obedience, he would have missed his miracle.

What is God telling you to let go of but your fists are closed tightly around it? Don't be afraid. Believe. Your story may end up different than what you hoped for, but you won't miss your miracle.

Prayer

God, I love how powerful control makes me feel. But that isn't Your goal for me. You want me to surrender to You so I don't miss out on Your best. You are writing a beautiful story for me, and Your plan is far better than anything I could achieve on my own. God, I don't want to miss out on what You have in store for me because I'm too scared to trust You. I'm letting go, opening my hands, and placing all my hope in You. In Jesus's name, amen.

~ Day 28 ~

Waiting

Good morning, beautiful!

I'm not very good at waiting. I prefer quick fixes.

The other day I was in my car, sitting too long at an intersection, when a car pulled out in front of me. I threw a fit. When my cell phone rang, I calmed down enough to answer. The caller was a good friend of mine who was driving that car! She laughed hysterically at my pointless road rage. I was totally embarrassed.

Everything in life takes time. We live in a fast-paced culture, but God runs in His own time zone. He doesn't look for quick fixes. With Him, it's not about the destination but the journey.

Waiting is part of how we grow our faith in God. In the waiting season is when I most often see God show up. Maybe that's because I've taken the time to look for Him rather than just living in the mundane.

In Hebrews 11:39-40, it says,

These were all commended for their faith, yet none of them

received what had been promised, since God had planned something better for us so that only together with us would they be made perfect.

Read the whole chapter of Hebrews 11. Every person who lived "by faith" had to go through a season of waiting. By this they became known by their faith.

If we stop striving for the destination, we will learn how to enjoy the journey. Through what feels like delays, God is fulfilling His promise for those coming after us. Our waiting unites us to the body of Christ as we live out His perfect plan.

Maybe God is cultivating something in you during this time that you will need in the future, and without it you would have missed it. Waiting is never wasted. It can be the fulfillment of the promise to come.

Let's learn how to enjoy the waiting together.

Prayer

God, delays can feel like a nuisance, but I know it is a gift from You to help grow my faith. Remind me that my waiting is not wasted but is part of Your perfect plan. Show me how to enjoy today. What can I learn from You in this time that I would have missed out on otherwise? Cultivate in me now what I am going to need in the future. Thank You for using this season to bring fulfillment of Your promises. In Jesus's name, amen.

~ Day 29 ~

A Beautiful Pursuit

Good morning, beautiful!

There's a longing in my heart to be wanted and loved unconditionally. My soul craves someone who will stop at nothing to chase me down if I run and fight for my love no matter what it takes.

The book of Hosea is a beautiful story of a man pursuing his wife. God told Hosea to marry Gomer, a prostitute. He loved her, married her, had children with her, and then she left him to return to prostitution. God told Hosea to find his wife and buy her back from her enslavement. He did. Hosea never stopped pursuing Gomer's heart.

The Lord said to me, "Go show your love to your wife again, though she is loved by another man and is an adulteress. Love her as the Lord loves the Israelites, though they turn to other gods and love the sacred raisin cakes." So I bought her for fifteen shekels of silver and about a homer and a lethek of barley. (Hosea 3:1–2)

Every time I read this story, I realize I am Gomer. God set me free, but I keep running back into the things that enslave me. I want to be loved by others, but I run when someone tries to show me love. I long for someone to pursue my heart like Hosea pursued Gomer, but I forget that someone already has. His name is Jesus.

Jesus chases me down every time I try to run. He will show me I'm loved no matter what it takes. He will stop at nothing in the pursuit of my heart. Jesus went to the cross to show me I am His. He redeemed me.

Beautiful one, if a longing inside you says you need someone to love you, what you are really searching for is Jesus. He has already paid the price for you, and He continues to pursue your heart every day. When your soul starts craving, remember that God is chasing after you.

Your desire to be pursued can never be filled by any human being. Only Jesus can do that.

I will plant her for myself in the land; I will show my love to the one I called "Not my loved one." I will say to those called "Not my people," "You are my people"; and they will say,

"You are my God." (Hosea 2:23)

Prayer

God, thank You for pursuing my heart every day. Help me to stop running from You and return to You. Fill me with more of You. Never stop reminding me of the love You have for me. In Jesus's name, amen.

~ Day 30 ~

Planted

Good morning, beautiful!

Over the years, many of my friends have moved away, married, and gone on to do great things. I'm still living in the same town. Sometimes I feel stuck and question myself. Am I doing what God called me to do? Shouldn't I be furtherer along than I am? Then God reminds me that He has placed me right where He wants me. This place and this season have a purpose. I am exactly where I'm supposed to be. Just because my story seems to be taking longer to tell, that doesn't mean it's unfinished.

Farmers know if a fruit or vegetable is picked too early it will lose potency or flavor. Waiting for the right time results in better-tasting food.

It's hard to tell if a seed is growing until you see the sprout emerging from under the soil. But just because you can't see the seed, that doesn't mean it isn't growing.

Sing about a fruitful vineyard; I, the Lord, watch over it; I water it continually. I guard it day and night so that no one may harm it. (Isaiah 27:2–3)

Do you feel buried? God has planted you right where He wants you to be. In this season of life, you are destined to have the greatest impact.

Sometimes it's hard to understand why things have happened to us or to others. We need to trust that God has planted us in the right season, at the right time, according to His plan. Our heavenly Father hasn't stopped tending the garden in which He has planted us. Soon we will feel sunlight shining on our faces. And the harvest will be plentiful!

So let your roots grow deep where you have been planted. Your heavenly Father will continue to watch, water, and guard your life. Remember, you story isn't finished.

Prayer

God, thank You for blessing me with this season I'm in. I believe You have planted me here intentionally. I know there is a purpose in this time of waiting that is greater than what I can see.

Remind me that You are still working in me. Preparing me now for what's ahead. Thank You for continuing to work in me even when I can't see the results. I will continue to place my trust in You. In Jesus's name, amen.

~ Day 31 ~

He > Me

Good morning, beautiful!

I have a desire deep inside for my name to be great and for the world to know and love me. Fame and fortune hold a sweet appeal to my soul. Yet my name means nothing unless it points others to a name that is greater than mine. I can live in a way that makes my name great, or I can live to make the name of Jesus greater.

I know this life is nothing unless it's lived for the glory of God. But in the moment, the idea of living for myself seems so much better. How can I move past my earthly desires and live for the one who fills my life with purpose, who has always been there for me, and has provided for all my needs? How can I move past my selfish ambition and honor the name of Jesus, who gave it all for me?

Whoever wants to be my disciple must deny themselves and take up their cross daily and follow me. For whoever wants to save their life will lose it, but whoever loses their life for me will save it. What good is it for someone to gain the whole world, and yet lose or forfeit their very self? (Luke 9:23–25)

Daily we must choose to deny ourselves and pick up our cross. Denying ourselves means setting aside our desires and dreams and putting others first. Taking up our cross means bearing the circumstances in our lives in a way that give Jesus glory.

He must become greater, I must become less. (John 3:30)

I work with middle and high school students, and I love watching this verse modeled in their lives. One of my students, Dixson, is a very talented musician. He is in twelfth grade and plays guitar in the band at our church. He could go far and easily make his name great through the eyes of the world. But Dixson never seeks for his name to be praised.

Instead, when no one is watching, He spends private time with God. In public, he invests in the lives of his friends and invites them to church. On days when he's out of school, he serves at the church. Dixson sends Scripture passages to his friends daily to encourage them.

Dixson has learned at a young age how to put God first in everything. He is not seeking for his name to be known but for the name of Jesus to be known to those around him. It's evident in all he does.

He is a manager in our local grocery store, where he invests in the lives of customers and coworkers, pointing them to Jesus. As Dixson is promoted, he promotes Jesus.

We must daily choose whose name we want to magnify. Do you want to make your name great? Or do you want to make His name great?

Prayer

God, You must become greater and I must become less. I don't want to work so hard building my own kingdom that I miss out on the greatest blessing of life: giving glory back to You. Because at the end of this life, Your name is the only one that matters. May my life tell the story of how great You are! In Jesus's name, amen.

~ Day 32 ~

Wonder

Good morning, beautiful!

A few months ago, I realized my faith journey had grown stale. Every day felt like a chore. I was following God just to check a box and get a pat on the back for being a good Christian. In reality, I hated that life. I wanted to walk away from my dream of letting the world know about Jesus. After all, was my work truly worth the effort?

One day it hit me. I had lost the wonder of following Jesus.

The word *wonder* carries a sense of admiration caused by something beautiful. It ignites discovery and passion. When wonder is gone, life becomes dull, following God seems like a chore, and we forget what it feels like to enjoy our daily adventure with Christ.

Sometimes we get caught up in thinking that God needs us to serve Him. God doesn't need us to do anything for Him. He created the whole universe in six days, without anyone's assistance. He has everything under control.

Yet He allows us to serve Him and take part in His grand

plans because He desires to teach us how to enjoy the wonder of His presence.

Imagine a dad taking his little girl to a field of daisies. They look at each one and notice how they are uniquely created. They marvel at the detail, and they delight in their time spent together. The little girl giggles as her daddy chases her through the meadow. She discovers the wonder of her father's pursuit. What if our relationship with God is meant to look like that? Reveling in our Father's pursuit of our hearts and marveling at His goodness? Discovering new meaning in the word *wonder* every moment of every day?

Beautiful one, have you lost your wonder? Pray for it again. Allow yourself to spend time with God in new ways. Here are a few suggestions to try. Spend time in nature, pay attention to what's around, and thank God. Listen to worship music while washing the dishes. Dance under the stars to God alone. Drive somewhere with no set destination and talk to God. Pull your Bible out again a started reading through one of the Gospels of Mathew, Mark, Luke, or John.

God longs to reignite wonder within you once again. As you discover your Father's heart, this sense of wonder will lead you to do great things for Him. Not out of obligation or need, but as an overflow of your heart. Go on a journey of wonder as you look at God through the eyes of a child.

Jesus said, "Let the little children come to me, and do not hinder them, for the kingdom of heaven belongs to such as these." (Matthew 19:14)

Prayer

God, reignite the sense of wonder in my soul. Create in me a childlike faith and nurture it to grow. I'm sorry for the times I've just checked the box on following You and forgot about the relationship. Don't stop pursuing my heart. Teach me to marvel at Your goodness to me. Fill my heart to overflowing with You so I may pour out that love on those around me. In Jesus's name, amen.

~ Day 33 ~

The Giver

Good morning, beautiful!

Author Jay Wolf, in a talk he gave at Passion City Church, said something that really spoke to me:

Sometimes it's like God is asking us, "What is it that you want from Me in this relationship? Do you just want Me to give you the good gifts that I will give you if you say the right words or do the right things? Or do you want to know the Giver of every good and perfect gift? That's what I'm offering you; it is Myself, not these outcomes. Do you want to stop hurting or do you want to know the Healer of the World?"[i]

So often I follow God based on what's in it for me, what I can get out of it. But I should be fixated on better knowing the Giver of every good and perfect gift: "the Father of the heavenly lights, who does not change like shifting shadows" (James 1:17). Check out the verse from the beginning of the chapter:

> Consider it pure joy, my brothers and sisters, whenever you face trials of many kinds, because we know that the testing of your faith produces perseverance. Let perseverance finish its work so that you may be mature and complete, not lacking anything. (James 1:2-4)

You can't truly appreciate the gift until you learn to know the one who's giving it. I say I want to know God more, but when a trial comes my way rather than using it to draw me closer to Him, I realize my desire all along was for the gift, not the Giver. When my attention is on receiving what I want, I miss an opportunity to have an encounter that will draw me closer to God.

Beautiful one, are you chasing the gift or the Giver?

Prayer

God, I'm sorry for all the times I wanted the gift more than I wanted You. Help me learn to know You. Use the trials that come my way to produce perseverance in me. And through that perseverance may I discover You, the one who desires to lavish good and perfect gifts on His beloved daughter—me. In Jesus's name, amen.

~ Day 34 ~

Fight for You

Good morning, beautiful!

There are days when my heart aches over previous hurts, disappointments, failures, and mistakes. I want to move on, but I feel like I keep taking one step forward and three steps back. I pray over and over, "Lord, help me to let go and move forward. Show me what I can do." But Scripture tells me:

The Lord will fight for you; you need only to be still.
(Exodus 14:14)

After leaving Egypt, the Israelites were faced with a seemingly impossible situation. In front of them was the Red Sea; behind them Pharaoh and the Egyptian army were coming to attack. Before God spilt the sea right down the middle to let the people walk to safety, Moses told the Israelites what they needed to do to move forward. He told them to "be still" because the Lord would fight for them.

I haven't learned very well how to let God fight for me. I tend to try to handle things myself. Yet I can't solve my problems or anyone else's.

Are there times when God calls us to fight along with Him? Absolutely! But there comes a time when we don't have the strength. That's when He whispers in our ears, "Be still." And then He runs straight into the war zone and takes care of the battle for us.

Beautiful one, what are you fighting? Is the battle draining every ounce of your strength? Maybe it's time for you to be still and let God lead the way. I'm not telling you to give up but rather to place your situation in the hands of the one who holds the world. He wants to help you move forward, but that can only happen if you let go and trust that He is going to take care of it for you. Will you surrender and let Him fight for you?

Prayer

God, You know what I am facing right now, and You know it's too big for me to defeat. I need You to fight for me. Help me to let go of past hurts, disappointments, failures, and mistakes. You have them all under control and they're in Your hands. I surrender them to You. Teach me to be still and allow You to do this with me.

Then lead me as I move forward. In Jesus's name, amen.

~ Day 35 ~

Burden Bearer

Good morning, beautiful!

If you suffer for doing good and endure it patiently, God is pleased with you. For God called you to do good even if it means suffering, just as Christ suffered for you. He is your example, and you must follow in his steps. (1 Peter 2:20–21 NLT)

The book of Amos is not the most uplifting portion of the Bible. In fact, it is pretty depressing. Amos was a sheep breeder when God called him to prophesy over the people of Israel. His message wasn't filled with joyful encouragement but rather a nightmare just waiting to happen.

The name Amos means "burden bearer." That's not a title I'd want to have! But sometimes God calls us to bear the burden of the work of Christ.

We have to put ourselves in the shoes of the people around

us. We walk with a friend through difficult times. We see those we love living in sin and we pray for them to have an encounter with Jesus. We invest in the lives of the people who haven't met God yet.

Rejoice inasmuch as you participate in the sufferings of Christ, so that you may be overjoyed when his glory is revealed. If you are insulted because of the name of Christ, you are blessed, for the Spirit of glory and of God rests on you. (1 Peter 4:13–14)

What if God wants to show us a different side of who He is? Is it possible to truly understand the love Jesus has for us without experiencing any of the burdens and suffering He faced? What if we are made more like Christ by bearing burdens? What if we see God's glory and blessing in the midst of suffering?

God calls all of us to minister in different ways. If we are entrusted to bear a small portion of the burden Christ took on for us, what an honor!

In the midst of the suffering, we get a greater glimpse of God's love for humanity. Sharing in a small portion of what Jesus did for us.

Ask God to let the burdens He places on your heart spark a passion within you to make a difference in your community and the world. Then look for what He wants to reveal to you as you go about your day.

The Lord your God is with you, the Mighty Warrior who saves. He will take great delight in you; in his love he will no longer rebuke you, but will rejoice over you with singing. (Zephaniah 3:17)

When the burden feels overwhelming, remember that the Lord your God is with you. He is the Mighty Warrior who saves, delights, loves, and rejoices with you in the good times and the difficult moments.

As you carry the weight of the burden God has called you to bear, ask Him for the strength you need to make it through. Ask Him to give you everything you need for the task at hand.

Prayer

God, what breaks Your heart the most? And what can I do about it with the resources You have given me? Use me to make a difference in my community and in the world. Equip me with the strength I need to do this. Thank You for entrusting me with this honor. In Jesus's name, amen.

~ Day 36 ~

Death of a Dream

Good morning, beautiful!

What do you do when a dream dies? What do you do when the hopes you had for your future have faded away and you know they will never become reality? How do you handle the heartbreak?

Andy Stanley, senior pastor of North Point Community Church, says:

Even if your heart is broken, it doesn't mean you're broken. Even when your dreams can't come true, it doesn't mean that God doesn't have a significant purpose for you. When your heart is broken and your dreams can't come true, that's our cue not to run, not to manipulate, not take matters into our own hands, not to reach for Goliath's sword, but to lean in, look up, and reach out to the God who has your whole world in His hands. That's the time to pray, "Heavenly Father, I offer You my dreams and plans. Do to me whatever seems good to You. I acknowledge Your right to rule. Your will be done in me. I offer You my dreams and plans because You care. Do to me whatever seems good to You. I acknowledge Your right to rule. Your will be done in me."[ii]

Even if your story doesn't look exactly like you expect, you can trust that His plans for you are good.

Even Jesus had to choose to trust in God's plans for Him when His disciples abandoned Him right before the crucifixion.

He withdrew about a stone's throw beyond them, knelt down and prayed, "Father, if you are willing, take this cup from me; yet not my will, but yours be done." (Luke 22:41-42)

Even if you are trusting that God's plans for you are good, it's okay to grieve the death of a dream. Go ahead and tell God how frustrated you are that this didn't happen. It's not a sin to feel the pain of heartbreak when every second hurts so deeply.

Give yourself time to mourn the loss, but don't let yourself stay there forever. Ask God what He is calling you to do next. Trust God with the dreams you have yet to see. When you reach this place of surrender, God can start a new work in you, preparing your heart for what's to come. New dreams are born as we humble ourselves enough to be moldable in our Father's hand.

Beautiful one, if your heart is breaking now, my heart is breaking with you. I know the pain that rises from the death of a dream. Remember, your story isn't over. It's just being remolded in the hands of our loving Father. He wants to ignite a new dream in you, and He has your best interests at heart. I know it's hard to see right now. But if you remain faithful, you will discover a new story that you wouldn't want to miss.

Prayer

Heavenly Father, I offer You my dreams and plans. Do to me whatever seems good to You. I acknowledge Your right to rule my life. May Your will be done in me. I offer You my dreams and plans because I know You care. In Jesus's name, amen.

~ Day 37 ~

Stop Running and Meet Your God

Good morning, beautiful!

I've been spending some time studying the Old Testament. I read about how God's chosen people, the Israelites, ran from Him over and over. I question why they continued running from such a good God who provided for their needs. Then I realize I am a runner too—not physically, but emotionally, relationally, and spirituality. When things get hard or I feel some sort of pain, I want to run as far and as fast as I can rather than turning to God. I run from His love, forgiveness, and grace because I get scared, and running feels safer.

"I gave you empty stomachs in every city and lack of bread in every town, yet you have not returned to me," declares the Lord. "I also withheld rain from you when the harvest was still three months away. I sent rain on one town, but withheld it from another. One field had rain; another had none and dried up. People staggered from town to town for water but did not get enough to drink, yet you have not returned to me," declares the Lord. (Amos 4:6–8)

Five times in this chapter, I see this phase "yet you have not returned to me." Apparently I'm not the only runner.

Why do we run from God's love, forgiveness, and grace? I think we run when we know we've messed up. We're ashamed of what we've done so we try to hide from God. We think we can fix it on our own. But this pattern is exhausting and ultimately leaves us more lost than when we started.

"Therefore this is what I will do to you, Israel, and because I
will do this to you, Israel, prepare to meet your God." He
who forms the mountains, who creates the winds, and who
reveals his thoughts to mankind, who turns dawn to darkness,
and treads on the heights of the earth—the Lord God
Almighty is his name. (Amos 4:12–13)

There is hope for us runners because we have a God who doesn't give up on us. Even when we have our "yet you have not returned to me" moments, He doesn't stop chasing us.

If we stop running, we will discover He's been with us the whole time. When we allow God to meet us where we are at we discover unrelenting love, unconditional forgiveness, and redeeming grace. Beautiful one, please stop running.

Prayer

God, when I mess up, I try to run from You. I attempt to fix the problem on my own, but all I really need is You. Help me to stop running. I want Romans 15:13 to be true for me: "May the God of hope fill you with all joy and peace as you trust in him, so that you may overflow with hope by the power of the Holy Spirit." In Jesus's name, amen.

~ Day 38 ~

I Lack Nothing

Good morning, beautiful!

The Lord is my shepherd, I lack nothing. (Psalm 23:1)

I love this verse. But I have to admit, I do lack something: contentment. My brain hears, "When you put your trust in God and follow Him, you will lack no good thing," and I know it's true, but my heart has a hard time believing it. I find myself in a daily tug-of-war where I believe the verse above and the next second I doubt if it is true because I don't feel content inside. I can't help wondering if God is forgetting something. Because showing up to another wedding single feels like I'm lacking. Not getting the job promotion feels like God missed something. Receiving another college rejection letter feels hopeless. Watching doors open for other people and stay closed for me feels like God hasn't followed through on His promises.

Paul writes:

I have learned to be content whatever the circumstances. I know what it is to have plenty. I have learned the secret of being content in any and every situation, whether well fed or hungry, whether living in plenty or in want. I can do all things through him who gives me strength. (Philippians 4:11–13)

I have to constantly remind myself that I am not God. He is much stronger and more capable than I can imagine. He delights in taking care of me. Yet my definition of "lacking nothing" and His are different.

The reason I lack confidence in my Shepherd is there is sometimes a gap between what I expect and what I experience. I expect to be well fed, but sometimes He lets me go hungry. I expect to live in plenty, but sometimes He leaves me in want. When my experiences don't match my expectations, I think my Shepherd has fallen short when it comes to taking care of me. Or maybe my problem is too big for Him to handle. But neither of those is accurate. The truth is, God is teaching me what it means to lack nothing and how I can find strength in my Savior.

The lions may grow weak and hungry, but those who seek the Lord lack no good thing. (Psalm 34:10)

Our Good Shepherd wants to teach us that when we seek Him, He will provide—whether that means we live in plenty or in want. When we change our perspective and learn to be content we began to understand how He is shaping us to be able to say in all circumstances, "I lack nothing."

Prayer

God, thank You for teaching me the value of being content in every season in life. Whatever I may face, I will lack nothing because my hope is in You. I surrender to You, my Good Shepherd. Show me what it means to lack nothing, whether I'm living in plenty or in want. Remind me that You always take good care of me. In Jesus's name, amen.

~ Day 39 ~

Accepted

Good morning, beautiful!

I feel pressured to earn acceptance from others and from God. I constantly wonder if I measure up. I feel like I have to prove that I am worthy of love. Underneath all this, what I'm really asking is "If everything fades around me, will others still find value in who I am? Does God accept me no matter what?"

When one of the Pharisees invited Jesus to have dinner with him, he went to the Pharisee's house and relined at the table. A women in that town who lived a sinful life learned that Jesus was eating at the Pharisee's house, so she came there with an alabaster jar of perfume. As she stood behind him at his feet weeping, she began to wet his feet with her tears. Then she wiped them with her hair, kissed them and poured perfume on them. (Luke 7:36–38)

This woman walked into a room where she knew everyone

there knew the mistakes of her past. Yet she didn't let that stop her, because she had found what she'd been searching for: Jesus. She went straight to Him, weeping, and poured the fragrant perfume from her alabaster jar onto His feet.

When the Pharisee who had invited him saw this, he said to himself, "If this man were a prophet he would know who is touching him and what kind of woman she is—that she is a sinner." Jesus answered him, "Simon, I have something to tell you." (Luke 7:39–40)

The woman's heart didn't matter to these Pharisees. All they could see were her mistakes. She didn't get any acceptance from them.

Look what Jesus says next.

He turned toward the woman and said to Simon, "Do you see this woman? I came into your house. You did not give me any water for my feet, but she wet my feet with her tears and wiped them with her hair. You did not give me a kiss, but this women, from the time I entered, has not stopped kissing my feet. You did not put oil on my head, but she has poured perfume on my feet. Therefore, I tell you, her many sins have been forgiven—as her great love has shown. But whoever has been forgiven little loves little."

Then Jesus said to her, "Your sins are forgiven."

The other guest began to say among themselves, "Who is this that even forgives sins?"

Jesus said to the woman, "Your faith has saved you; go in peace." (Luke 7:44–50)

Jesus didn't reject this woman because of her mistakes. He didn't chastise her for interrupting a dinner where she wasn't invited. He didn't reject her demonstration of love for Him. He healed all of the wounds from her past with love and acceptance.

Pouring perfume on Jesus's feet didn't earn His acceptance or forgiveness—it had already been given. This was an act of gratitude that Jesus wanted to forgive and accept her, despite everything.

She'd walked into a place where she wasn't accepted, and

Jesus told her to leave in peace.

I think Jesus taught someone else a lesson on acceptance in this moment as well. Simon the Pharisee should have had it all together. He was supposed to teach others how to follow God. But at his own party, right there in front of his friends, the King of kings corrected him.

After Jesus told the woman to "go in peace," Scripture doesn't say Jesus left because Simon messed up. Instead of rejecting him, Jesus corrected, forgave, and accepted Simon, flaws and all, and stayed to enjoy the dinner party.

I am more like that woman and Simon than I'd like to admit. Yet I am grateful that God accepts the best and worst versions of me.

I don't have to seek the acceptance of others. I can experience freedom and forgiveness when I run weeping to the feet of Jesus. There I find I have all I need: His acceptance, His forgiveness, and His love. I don't have to earn those things because they have already been given. The pieces of my heart that have been torn and tattered by others can go in peace.

Beautiful one, God accepts the best and worst versions of you. Stop searching for acceptance from others. At Jesus's feet you will discover you already have everything you need.

Prayer

God, I want to stop seeking the acceptance of others and run to You. Remind me that You accept me no matter what. I come to Your feet weeping. Striving to measure up will stop when I let You show me that I have all that I need in You. I don't have to earn it; You give it unconditionally every day. In Jesus's name, amen.

~ Day 40 ~

Fragrant Incense

Good morning, beautiful!

Two words have been rolling around in my head the past few weeks: *fragrance* and *incense*. According to the *Lexico English Dictionary*, incense is "a gum, spice, or other substance that is burned for the sweet smell it produces."[iii] A fragrance is "a pleasant, sweet smell."[iv] The common tie I see is the sweet smell they both produce.

> May my prayer be set before you like incense; may the lifting up of my hands be like the evening sacrifice. Set a guard over my mouth, Lord; keep watch over the door of my lips. Do not let my heart be drawn to what is evil so that I take part in wicked deeds along with those who are evildoers; do not let me eat their delicacies. (Psalm 141:2-4)

Our lives are like incense to the Lord. Every day as we face trials and experience joy, we are burned, and a smell is released from the character of our lives. Our truest character is revealed when we walk through the fire.

What smell is being released from your words, actions, decisions, and leadership? Is it a fragrant, sweet aroma or a stench that could foul an entire room?

The past thirty-nine days we have been redefining the way we see ourselves to align more with the way God sees us. When we allow Him to transform us, the way we treat those around us changes as well.

Change can be a painful process. But if you let God take charge of your life, it will be a fragrant incense that lets the world see Jesus through you.

Ask God to guard your lips so the words you say build others up. Ask Him to guard your heart so you can refrain from doing what is wrong and live in a way that pleases Him.

Beautiful one, God created you to live a purposeful life. He wants to make every broken piece of you whole. Are you willing to give Him control of your life, as an offering of fragrant incense to the one who gave everything for you?

The fig tree forms its early fruit; the blossoming vines spread their fragrance. Arise, come, my darling; my beautiful one, come with me. (Song of Songs 2:13)

Prayer

God, I want You to take every insecurity, fear, doubt, and rejection I've experienced and use them to bring me closer to You so I can reach a place of healing. Make my life a fragrant incense for Your name. I'm grabbing hold of Your hand, ready to follow You on the adventure of a lifetime. Thank You for breathing new life inside me. In Jesus's name, amen.

My beloved spoke and said to me, "Arise, my darling, my beautiful one, come with me. See! The winter is past; the rains are over and gone. Flowers appear on the earth; the season of singing has come, the cooling of doves is heard in our land. The fig tree forms its early fruit; the blossoming vines spread their fragrance. Arise, come, my darling; my beautiful one, come with me."

(Song of Songs 2:10–13)

Thank you for coming on the journey with me!

If you would like to take a next step on your faith journey and begin following Jesus this is for you!

First Step: Admit that God has not been first place in my life; ask Him to forgive your sins.

"But if we confess our sins, he will forgive our sins, because we can trust God to do what's right. He will cleanse us from all the wrongs we have done." 1 John 1:9 (NCV)

Second Step: Believe that Jesus died to pay for your sins. He rose again and is alive today.

If you declare with your mouth, 'Jesus is Lord,' and believe in your heart that God raised Jesus from the dead, you will be saved." Romans 10:9 (NCV)

"Salvation is found in no one else, for there is no other name under heaven given to mankind by which we must be saved." Acts 4:12

Third Step: Accept God's free gift of salvation. Do not try to earn it! Our relationship to God is not restored by anything we do, but on the basis of what Jesus has already done for us!

"For it is by grace you have been saved, through faith —and this not from yourselves, it is the gift of God— not by works, so that no one can boast." Ephesians 2:8-9

Fourth Step: Invite Jesus Christ to come into your life and be the director "Lord" of your life.

"Jesus says, 'Here I am! I stand at the door and knock. If anyone hears my voice and opens the door, I will come in...'" Revelation 3:20

About the Author

Katie has spent most of her life investing in teenagers. She works as a student director in her local community. She has spoken frequently at local middle & high schools.

Katie has watched countless young women sell themselves short because they have listened to the lies of their insecurities rather than the truth of God's word. Through counseling young women this is the daily encouragement Katie desires young women to hear.

End Notes

[i] Jay and Katherine Wolf, "Suffer Strong," Passion City Church, August 18, 2019, https://passioncitychurch.com/gathering/suffer-strong/.

[ii] Andy Stanley, "Getting Over a Broken Heart," *Love, Dates & Heartbreaks* part 6, https://yourmove.is/videos/love-dates-heartbreaks-part-6-getting-over-a-broken-heart/.

[iii] *Lexico English Dictionary* (Oxford University Press, 2020), s.v. "incense," https://www.lexico.com/en/definition/incense.

[iv] *Lexico English Dictionary* (Oxford University Press, 2020), s.v. "fragrance," https://www.lexico.com/en/definition/fragrance.

Made in the USA
Columbia, SC
07 August 2023

21173758R00074